THE NOTHING

BY SAL MURDOCCA

CROWN PUBLISHERS, INC. NEW YORK

To CAROLINE, my friend

Published by Crown Publishers, Inc.,
One Park Avenue, New York, New York 10016
and simultaneously in Canada
by General Publishing Company Limited
Manufactured in The Netherlands

Library of Congress Cataloging in Publication Data
Murdocca, Sal.
The nothing.
Summary: Melissa finds something that seems to
be neither animal, vegetable, nor mineral, yet it
becomes a loved member of the family.
1. Children's stories, American.   I. Title.
PZ7.M94No   1985   [E]   84-11428
ISBN 0-517-55535-2
10 9 8 7 6 5 4 3 2 1
First Edition

Louis was playing ball with his friends in the backyard. His sister, Melissa, came running.

"Louis!" she called excitedly. "I found something in the woods!"

Louis looked annoyed. "What is it?"

"I don't know," said Melissa, "but it's something, and it's very large."

Melissa led the boys a short way into the woods.

"There!" she said, pointing to a large round shape, partially hidden in the bushes.

Louis and his friends approached it slowly.

"What is it?" asked Melissa.

"I don't know," replied Louis.

One of the boys gently poked it.

"It's soft like clay," he said.

Another boy gave it a squeeze.

"And it's so fat," he said.

Another boy sniffed it.

"It doesn't smell," he said.

The last boy jumped on it.

"It's nothing," he said. "Let's go back and play."

Louis and his friends started to walk away.

Melissa began to cry. "It is *so* something! I want to take it home."

Louis carried it into the backyard. It weighed no more than a feather. The boys started tossing it around like a beach ball.

Suddenly the thing cried out, "HELP!"

"STOP!" shouted Melissa.

One of the boys let it fall to the ground.

Everyone stood staring at the thing.

"Are you all right?" asked Melissa.

"Much better, thank you," said the thing. "I was getting very dizzy."

"Who are you?" asked Louis.

"I don't know," replied the thing.

"Where did you come from?" asked Melissa.

"I don't remember," said the thing.

"Are you an animal, vegetable, or mineral?" asked a boy.

"I don't know." The thing began to cry.

"It's stupid," said the boy.

"It is not!" shouted Melissa. "It's just lost."

Melissa called her mother.

Her mother stared at the thing. "It doesn't look like anything I know," she said. "We'll ask your father when he gets home."

"Can we take it in the house?" said Melissa.

"I don't see why not," said her mother.

That evening the children greeted their father at the door. "We found something, but we don't know what it is."

"Well, let's have a look," said their father.

When their father saw the thing he scratched his head and said, "I really don't know what that is."

"It must be something," said Melissa.

"Everything is something," said Louis.

"I'm sure you're right," said their father. "But it looks like nothing I've ever seen."

"What if it *is* nothing?" said their mother. "What do you do with nothing?"

"Let's take it to the zoo," said Louis.

"They'll know what it is," said Melissa.

"I hope so," said the nothing.

The next morning, which was a Saturday, the family drove to the City Zoo. The nothing sat in the back seat with the children.

"What is this?" asked the nothing.

"This is a car," said Melissa.

The zookeeper looked at the nothing. He poked it, squeezed it, tickled it, and took its temperature.

"I've never seen anything like this," said the zookeeper. "I think we should show it to the Zoological Society."

The doctors at the National Zoological Society performed many tests on the nothing. They poked it, squeezed it, took its temperature, weighed it, and X-rayed it. When they were finished, their president said, "We have performed all the tests. As far as we can see, it is not an animal."

"It must be something," said Melissa.

That evening the family had a long talk.

"Maybe it's a vegetable," said Louis, petting the nothing.

"Let's bring it to a farmer," said Melissa.

On the following Saturday the family drove out into the country with the nothing sitting in the back seat.

The farmer looked at the nothing and scratched his beard. He poked it, squeezed and smelled it for freshness.

"As far as I can tell," said the farmer, "it is not a vegetable. Maybe it's a mineral."

A week later the family drove to the Museum of Natural History in the heart of the great city.

"Maybe you are a mineral," said Melissa, petting the nothing in the back seat.

"I hope not," said the nothing.

At the Museum of Natural History, the nothing was examined by experts of every kind. They poked it, squeezed it, weighed it, and X-rayed it.

When the tests were completed the curator said, "It is most certainly *not* a mineral."

The nothing began to cry.

"Don't cry," said Melissa. "Who wants to be a mineral anyway?"

Suddenly the curator had an idea. "Say, why don't you take it to an art museum? It may just be a work of art."

"Maybe you are a great work of art," said Melissa as they
walked up the long flight of stairs.

"I don't think so," said the nothing.

The head of the Metropolitan Museum of Art looked at the nothing. "It's very interesting. Very interesting. Who is the artist?" he asked.

"We don't know," said their mother.

"I found it," said Melissa.

"Hmmmm," said the head of the museum as he gave a little squeeze to the nothing's nose.

"OUCH!" said the nothing.

"Oh my goodness!" said the head of the museum. "It's alive!" Then he shook his head. "I'm afraid that this cannot be a work of art."

The family drove home in silence with the nothing sitting in the back seat looking out the window.

"Did I say something wrong?" asked the nothing.

"Of course not," said Melissa.

The next day two strange men appeared at their front door.

"We're from the FBI," said the tall thin man.

"That's right," said the short fat one. "We heard that you have something strange here."

The two men from the FBI questioned the nothing.

"Who are you?" said the tall thin man.

"I don't know," said the nothing.

"Where did you come from?" asked the other man.

"I don't remember," said the nothing.

"I'm afraid that we'll have to take you in for some more questioning," said the tall thin man.

The FBI men drove away with the nothing sitting in the back seat.

"I know that this is a car," said the nothing.

"Anything you say will be taken down as evidence and may be used against you," said the short fat FBI man writing in a small notebook.

The FBI investigated the case of the nothing for three days. On the fourth day the two FBI men returned with the nothing.

"It's all yours," said the short fat man to Melissa.

"Did you find out anything?" asked her father.

"Nothing at all," replied the tall thin man.

After several days, stories about the nothing started appearing in the newspapers. All day long reporters called on the telephone trying to talk with the nothing.

Finally the family gave permission to have the nothing appear on a nationally televised talk show. A contest was announced and the TV show offered a reward to anyone who could identify the nothing.

Thousands of people, with just as many guesses, replied.

One person said that it was a piece of the moon.

Another said it was a kind of jellyfish.

One jokester wrote in and said it was just a bunch of baloney.

After several weeks, the TV station announced that no one had won the contest.

The announcer said, "I'm afraid that all this fuss has been over nothing."

"You *are* something," said Melissa to the nothing.

After the excitement about the contest was over the nothing settled down to a normal life with Melissa and the family. After a while it was treated like just another member of the household.

Although the nothing never ate, it enjoyed sitting down with the family at dinner.

Although the nothing did not watch television, it liked to watch the family enjoying its favorite programs.

The nothing enjoyed going to the beach and floating in the water.

It also enjoyed being read to by Melissa.

The nothing even learned to enjoy being tossed around by the children in the backyard.

One evening, while everyone was asleep, a burglar came in and stole the nothing. A note arrived two days later.

It read: IF YOU WANT TO SEE THIS THING AGAIN, IT WILL COST YOU TEN THOUSAND DOLLARS.

The police were called in, and the story appeared in the newspapers and on television.

People all over the country were outraged and marched in protest over the kidnapping.

Weeks passed, but not a word was heard about the nothing.

"We'll have to pay the ransom," said Melissa. "I'll get a job."

But on the very next morning the nothing appeared on their doorstep. There was a note attached to it.

It read: PLEASE TAKE THIS THING BACK. I CAN'T EXPECT ANYONE TO PAY SOMETHING FOR NOTHING.

"But you *are* something," said Melissa.

Everyone was overjoyed to see the nothing again.

There was a grand parade in the city, and the nothing was awarded four prizes by the mayor.

The first award was a plaque from the National Zoological Society declaring the nothing to be an honorary animal.

The second award was a golden tag from the Farmers' Association declaring the nothing to be an honorary fresh vegetable.

The third presentation was a medal from the Museum of Natural History declaring the nothing to be an honorary mineral.

The fourth award was a document from the Metropolitan Museum of Art declaring the nothing was a genuine and priceless work of art.

"Perhaps I'm too much," said the nothing, laughing.

After the nothing had been with the family for a year, they decided to give it a birth date and threw a birthday party in its honor.

"We love you," said Melissa.

"And that makes you really something," said her mother.